# The Time Machine Girls

ERNESTINE TITO JONES

Jones, Ernestine Tito
The Time Machine Girls
Book Three: Courage
Website: www.ernestinetitojones.com

the Time Machine Girls

3

Courage

# Chapter One

Bess spun around the living room in her sparkly fairy outfit. The glittery wings attached to her back bounced up and down as she spun. "Guess how many times I've twirled around so far?" she asked.

Hazel didn't answer. She was getting dizzy just watching her little sister. She went back to the cute puppy puzzle she was working on at the coffee table. Her sister almost bumped into her as she twirled.

Bess stumbled to a stop. "If I counted right, I'm on a million gazillion and seven, but who knows? I really stopped counting after a million gazillion." She started spinning again. "A million gazillion and eight... A million gazillion and nine..."

Hazel rolled her eyes. She knew Bess was bored. She was bored too. Being stuck at their grandparents' farmhouse while they helped them move wasn't her idea of a fun summer. Her friends were probably going to an amusement park somewhere or heading out to a weeklong camping trip. Hazel had to watch her 6-year-old sister twirl around a living room. Ugh.

The only fun days they'd had so far were the ones when they got to use the time machine in the attic. She and Bess had gone back twice now. The first time they visited a young George Washington. The second time was a couple of days ago when they met Thomas Edison on the day he invented the light bulb.

That was also the day when everything had changed at the farmhouse. Their grumpy grandfather had turned out to be not so grumpy after all. Hazel actually thought he was pretty amazing. He had saved Bess's friendship bracelet for years when the girls lost it traveling through time. He let them know he knew they were using his time machine, and he not only seemed okay with it, he also told them he needed their help with it.

But that was where it had ended, and that was two days ago.

"I'm bored," Bess said, finally stopping herself from spinning. She stumbled across the room in a dizzy trance, her arms stretched out like Frankenstein. She giggled as she tripped over nothing, hitting the side table full of their grandmother's knickknacks. A small cat statue teetered this way and that, falling off the table.

Hazel reached over and caught it just before it landed on the floor. She shot Bess an angry glance. "Be careful, Bess, or I'll have to tell on you again," she said. Hazel hated being the only one who cared about the rules their mother gave them to follow. She hated being the one in charge.

"You promised you wouldn't tell on me anymore," Bess said, flopping onto the couch. She pulled at the glitter on the wing of her costume.

"And you promised to follow the

rules," Hazel reminded her. She thought about that one. Bess hadn't meant to knock the statue over. "I'm sorry," she said. "Just try to be careful."

Bess folded her arms and kicked her shiny ballet flat into the patterns of the faded green carpet. "Let's ask Grandpa when we can use the time machine again," she said.

Her pet frog was sitting in his plastic aquarium on the coffee table. She pulled him out and up to her face. "Froggenstein wants to go back in time again. Isn't that right, Froggenstein?"

Rrrrrrrrrrr-ibbbet!

Hazel grimaced, watching the frog germs being smeared across her sister's face. "I don't know," she replied. She pulled a small bottle of hand sanitizer from her back pocket. "Let's go outside and play something. It's finally not raining. We'll use the time machine whenever Grandpa says we can."

"Ask him when that'll be," Bess said.

"No, Bess. He told us a couple of days ago that he would let us know when it was safe."

"Maybe it's safe now," Bess replied, setting Froggenstein down on their grandparents' sofa. "You're not afraid to ask him, are you?"

"No," Hazel lied. "I just don't want to bug him about it, that's all." She knew Bess was right. Even though their grandfather wasn't as mean as she thought he was, Hazel was still a little afraid of him. He always seemed angry.

Bess giggled as Froggenstein hopped

across their grandparents' sofa.

Even though it wasn't officially against the rules, Hazel was pretty sure their grandparents weren't going to be happy about Bess putting her frog on their furniture. "Bess, you can't have Froggenstein out in the living room."

"Why do you always get to decide everything?" Bess asked, picking her frog up and putting him back in his carrier.

The ribbon in Hazel's hair fell along the side of her shoulder. She pulled it out and retied it, tighter this time. "Because I'm older," she explained, yanking at the strands of the red ribbon. "I wish I didn't have to be the one in charge, but Mom put me in charge while she helps Grandma and Grandpa."

Bess scrunched her face. "Okay, if

you're the one in charge then ask if we can go in the time machine again, unless you're chicken."

"I'm not chicken…" Hazel said, twirling a nervous finger into her ribbon.

"Good," replied Bess. "Then ask him. Ask Grandpa…"

"Ask me what?" a booming voice said. Both girls jumped. It was their grandfather. And like usual, he looked angry.

# Chapter Two

Bess ran up to their grandfather and gave him a huge hug. His thick eyebrows rose in surprise then softened with his wrinkles as he laughed. He didn't look nearly as angry or mean when he smiled. He just looked like a grandpa.

Neither of the girls really knew their grandparents very well. They'd only met them a few times and their mother didn't really talk about them. Hazel was starting to get used to her grandfather's grumpy looks and her grandmother's homemade food.

"Hazel has something she wants to ask you," Bess said to their grandfather, motioning to Hazel to go ahead and hurry up. Hazel bit her lip, trying to hide her fear.

Their grandfather sat down on the couch. "What is it? You can ask me anything."

Hazel looked at her spotless white tennis shoes as she spoke. "W-w-we were just wondering... hoping, really," she paused, trying to think of a way to say things.

Bess didn't give her a chance to finish. She flopped on the couch by their grandfather. "We were just wondering if we could use the time machine today."

"I'm glad you asked," their grandfather said to Bess. Hazel wished she'd have been the one brave enough to ask now that it seemed so easy.

Their grandfather continued. "It's why I came in here. I was looking for you to see if you'd like to return something in time today."

Bess shrugged. "What else are we going to do?"

Hazel threw her sister a look then turned back to their grandfather. "Are you coming too," Hazel asked. "It would be fun to go on an adventure together." Hazel also knew that if he went, she wouldn't have to be the one to keep her sister out of trouble. She wouldn't have to be the responsible one who made sure the rules got followed, again and again.

Their grandfather tugged on his shaggy beard like he was thinking about it. "No. I can't go this time," he said. "I'm afraid your mother would wonder where I was. She worries about me a lot because she thinks I'm crazy." He gave the girls a wink.

"Well, are you crazy?" Bess asked, running a hand through her messy blonde hair, making it even messier.

Hazel turned toward her sister. "Bess, that's not polite," she said, even though she wanted to know too. Hazel had always heard her grandfather was crazy. He didn't seem crazy, or at least not all the time.

"We can talk about our crazy family later," he said.

Hazel stopped herself from

reminding her grandfather that she was part of the family, and she wasn't crazy at all. She always tried to follow the rules and do everything perfectly.

"Let's talk about the time machine instead," their grandfather said. "Your grandmother and I haven't thought too much about it for a very long time, not until you two got here. We knew it was something that we needed to forget about."

"Why did you take those things from history?" Bess asked. Hazel shushed her sister, but looked at her grandfather to see if he'd answer the question.

Their grandfather's eyes looked tiny under the weight of his huge eyebrows, even though they were raised. "That's precisely why I need your help. We need to return those items. Maybe not all of them, but as many as we can before your grandmother and I move," he said. "We won't be able to take the time machine with us."

"What are you going to do with the time machine when you move?" Bess asked.

Their grandfather ignored Bess's question and instead talked about how to use the time machine, how the green button turned it on and how pushing the yellow one made it flash through time.

Hazel was hardly paying attention. She still had so many questions she wanted to ask her grandfather, but she couldn't get herself to do it. Last time she and Bess used the time machine to go back in time to visit Thomas Edison, they had also accidentally gone back in time to when their grandfather was a young professor about to demonstrate his time machine at a county fair. Their mother was just a kid back then, and she was very excited to become famous for having a time machine.

Hazel knew something terrible must have happened the day of the fair. Her grandparents were no longer professors, and their family was not famous for having a time machine.

She wanted to ask about that day. The day of the fair that had somehow changed everything.

She looked at her sister. Bess was busy bobbing her head and swinging her legs on the couch while their grandfather talked. Nothing bothered her, and she wasn't afraid to do or ask anything.

Hazel knew she needed to be more

like her sister.

"So that's the most important part. Understand?" their grandfather said.

Hazel gasped, realizing she hadn't heard a word.

"Wait. What? What about the fair?" Hazel blurted out.

# Chapter Three

Bess giggled so hard she fell over on the couch. "And you tell me I never listen."

Hazel's face went red.

Their grandfather turned his head to the side. Hazel could tell he was surprised she hadn't been paying attention because she was usually the responsible one.

Their grandfather coughed. "I was just telling you both how I made a decision on the next item you should return to history. It's already in a cloth bag in the trunk, a pair of boots this time. When you get to the house, tell Mr. Garrett you found them just outside the door in a box."

He talked slowly like he was making sure Hazel was listening. "That's the most important part. Understand?"

"Yes," Bess said, giving a thumbs-up. "We found Mr. Ferret's shoes in our trunk with some socks. Got it."

Hazel laughed nervously. Her face was still felt red from embarrassment. "Don't worry, Grandpa. I got it this time. We need to return the items to the house where Mr. Garrett lives." She turned to her sister. "But we can't tell them we got them in an old army trunk in the future, Bess. If he asks, we need to tell him we found them."

Their grandfather nodded. He seemed glad someone was actually listening this time. Warm sunlight shone in from the window in the living room, and their grandfather turned and looked outside. "Your grandmother, mother, and I are going to finish cleaning out the barn today. We'll be gone most of the afternoon. You can probably leave then. But I'll let you know if it's safe by giving you a wink. Got it? Our signal is a wink."

Hazel and Bess both gave him a hug. Even though it was a beautiful sunny day, Hazel couldn't wait to leave somewhere. The old farmhouse was pretty boring if she and Bess weren't using the time machine.

Their grandfather looked at his watch then quickly added. "Your grandmother packed you some homemade bread. I put it in the cloth bag, too, but don't eat it all. Take it to the group. They'll be hungry. Tell them your grandmother made it."

"Wait," Hazel said, surprised. "Grandma knows we've been using the time machine?"

Their grandfather's eyebrows shifted into slants again. "Of course she does. This time machine is both of ours. Your grandmother and I were..." He paused, looking off, out the window. "Before we took up the farm, your grandmother and I were both professors. We built the time machine together."

"Why did you stop being professors?" Bess asked.

"We'll get to all of that later," he said. His voice rose like he was getting angry again. "Don't let your mother know about the time machine," their grandfather said. Hazel waited for her sister to ask why. She didn't.

"And wear some warm clothes and good walking shoes," he added. He got up to leave just as Hazel heard her grandmother and mother come in through the kitchen door. Her grandmother was humming loudly. Hazel guessed that her grandmother was probably warning them that their mother was coming inside, so they would stop talking about the time machine.

Hazel wondered why she couldn't mention anything about the time machine to her mother. Was it all part of the family secret that happened the day of the fair?

"As soon as we go out to the barn, I'm pretty sure you'll be able to leave too," her grandfather said. He turned to the girls. "Thank you for helping me. Unless something weird happens, we'll be able to get these items returned to their proper spots in history in no time now that I have your help."

Their mom walked into the room and kissed each girl on the forehead. She was followed by their grandmother, and a red-haired boy in a baseball cap they'd never seen before. He was carrying a soccer ball.

"Girls, I want you to meet Bobby. He lives down the street. I grew up with Bobby's mother. He came over to play. Isn't that nice? Now you won't be bored anymore, at least not this afternoon." Their mother's smile was huge and encouraging.

Hazel looked over at Bess who looked over at their grandpa. They all knew what that meant. No one was going anywhere in the time machine with Bobby around.

# Chapter Four

Outside, Bobby kicked the soccer ball from one foot to the other. "I'm bored," he said, scowling. "My mom was the one who made me come over when she saw your mom again. I tried to tell her little kids were boring."

Bess turned her head to the side and frowned. "That's not very nice," she said.

Bobby shrugged. "So?" He kicked the ball to Bess. She reached her foot out to kick it back but missed. Bobby groaned.

"See? You're too little. I only came over because I heard from my mom that your grandparents were crazy, and I wanted to see for myself. Are they really crazy?"

"No. They're just regular grandparents," Hazel said. She felt her face growing redder by the minute. Her grandparents had a lot of secrets and a lot of rules, but they weren't crazy. Or at least, she didn't think they were.

"They do have a time machine," Bess said, matter-of-factly.

Bobby's eyes widened. "A what?" he asked. A smile formed along his round face.

Hazel elbowed her sister, and laughed loudly. "Little kids! They have the best imaginations," she said, still laughing. "I'm eight, and I wish I still had the imagination of a six-year-old."

*Why did her sister always say the wrong things at the wrong times?*

Bobby kicked the ball into the air with only his feet then he used his head and knees to keep it going. "So do you have to watch your little sister every day?" he asked Hazel. "That's no fun."

Hazel nodded and bit her lip. He was right. It wasn't fun all the time.

The sun was bright overhead and the air smelled like freshly cut grass. Their mom said it was the first beautiful day in a long time and they should play outside, but all Hazel and Bess wanted to do was go into the attic. Bobby kicked the ball to Hazel. She kicked it back. The new kid nodded approvingly. "You're good, not like your sister," he said. "I guess because you're older." He showed Hazel how to use the side of her foot to dribble the ball. He ran with the ball over to the old oak tree and back again. Then, he kicked it to Hazel.

Hazel tried her best to do it just the way he told her to. It was nice to have someone older to play with, someone she didn't have to take care of for a change.

"Wow!" he said, when Hazel kicked the ball back to him, but it went over his head. "You're better than most the kids on my team. That was some kick."

Hazel beamed. She looked over at Bess who wasn't watching them play soccer. She was sitting by a bush, digging in the dirt. "Do you want to play too?" Hazel asked her sister.

Bess didn't answer. She picked up a rock and checked underneath it. Hazel could tell her sister was mad at her, but she wasn't sure why. Bess ran her hand through the soil under the bush again.

"What are you doing?" Bobby asked her.

"Looking for bugs for my pet frog, Froggenstein," Bess replied. She proudly held up the aquarium with her frog in it. "I caught him all by myself. Isn't he beautiful? I think he's hungry."

Bobby stopped kicking the soccer ball around with Hazel and snatched the aquarium out of Bess's hand. "I'll take that. Little kids can't take care of frogs. You should give him to me and Hazel. We're older."

Bess's face dropped as Bobby held the cage high over his head. Hazel wanted to snatch it back from their new friend. Sure, her sister was annoying sometimes. And sure, she liked frog germs a little too much, but Froggenstein was her frog. Hazel kicked her feet into the grass of the backyard. She couldn't get herself to say any of that. She was afraid the new kid wouldn't like her if she stood up to him. She was afraid her mother would be mad at her if she said something because Bobby's mother was a family friend. Why was she always so afraid to say stuff?

Bess looked at Hazel for help. Her eyes seemed especially big under her thick glasses. Hazel swallowed hard. She knew she had to stand up for her sister. She knew she needed to say something.

# Chapter Five

The air felt thick and heavy, and Hazel had to remind herself to breathe. She reached for the aquarium. "L-l-look, Bobby," she stuttered. "This is Bess's frog, but maybe we can help you find a frog of your own."

"I already have a frog," he said, snatching the aquarium back. "But you two can help me find some food for him. He's hungry."

"Give it back, Bobby," Hazel said.

"I'll give it back later, after I see him eat something," he replied.

Bobby walked off toward the bushes where Bess had been looking for crickets before. He was still carrying her sister's frog.

Hazel didn't know what to do. She knew it was wrong for Bobby to take her sister's frog and she didn't want to look for bugs anyway. Was he telling the truth when he said he'd give the frog back after he fed him?

Hazel pretended to search the ground for crickets, kicking over rocks and dirt while she tried to think of a plan. Off in the distance, she saw the old red barn. She knew her mom and grandparents were busy cleaning it. She could easily run over and tell on Bobby, but then, he did say he was going to give the frog back. The sun beat down on her head, causing her face to sweat. She hated sweating. She hated bugs, and she didn't think her new friend was very nice either. Hazel's ribbon fell from her bun again. She went to pick it up and noticed a little cricket poking its head out from under a stick.

She jumped. "I think I found one, Bess!" she said. "I found a bug!"

Bobby ran over to Hazel. He set Froggenstein down by her feet. "Oh yeah. A juicy cricket. Killer will like that."

Had he already renamed her sister's frog? This was worse than she'd thought. He probably wasn't planning on giving the frog back.

Hazel looked around for her sister.

She knew she had to be mad. But Bess was nowhere to be found. Maybe she'd gone to the barn to tell on Bobby.

"Where's Bess?" she asked.

Bobby pounced on the cricket, scooping it into his thick freckled hands. "She said something about going by herself to play your grandpa's video game. She sounded crazy. Are you sure your family isn't crazy?"

*Did he just say Bess went by herself to their grandpa's video game?"* That meant the time machine!

The cricket jumped out of Bobby's hands, and he bent down to pick it up again. While Bobby was distracted, Hazel knew it was her chance. She grabbed Froggenstein and took off up to the house, looking back every once in a while to make sure Bobby wasn't following her. She needed to catch up to Bess, and fast.

"Hey! Where are you going with my frog?" He yelled, running after her toward the house.

She wanted to yell back that it wasn't his frog, but she just kept running.

As soon as she got to the backdoor, she raced inside. She could hear Bobby still yelling after her.

She closed the door and ran up the stairs. "Bobby wouldn't come into the house without asking, would he?" she wondered. "Maybe, but not up to the attic." She decided to take the stairs two at a time, just in case she was wrong. Her heart pounded underneath her t-shirt and she could hardly catch her breath. She hoped she wasn't already too late.

The old wooden stairs of their grandparents' farmhouse echoed under the weight of her feet as Hazel ran up them as fast as she could. Bess was too little to do this alone. Why hadn't she stood up for her sister sooner?

Just as she was about to open the attic door, she heard it. The familiar rumbling sounds of the time machine's engine. The floor began to rock under her feet.

Her hand shook at the knob. Could she make it in time?

# Chapter Six

The attic was dark and the light overhead flickered with the booming vibrations coming from the time machine off in the corner. Hazel knew she didn't have time to let her eyes adjust to the dim light. She stumbled forward through the darkness in the direction of the bookcase.

"Wait, Bess! Wait!" she called as loud as she could, hoping to see her sister and stop her from going anywhere by herself.

Somehow, Hazel managed to make it across the room without tripping on anything. She grabbed onto the bookcase to get her balance. Even though she couldn't really see, she knew the time machine was only a few feet away. Blinking wildly, she tried to force her eyes to adjust to the darkness. In the shadows of the attic, she saw her sister's face inside the time machine's domed plastic lid. Bess's eyes were swollen and red. She'd been crying, and Hazel knew it was all her fault.

Hazel waved an arm, trying to get her sister's attention. She held up the small plastic aquarium with the other.

Bess didn't seem to notice. She dramatically dabbed at her eyes with the short puffy sleeve of her fairy outfit then went to push a button on the control panel in front of her. Hazel couldn't believe her sister was actually planning on leaving without her!

Hazel quickly lunged for the time machine. Bess looked up when Hazel hit the side of it.

"Rrrrrrriiiiiiibbbet," went Froggenstein.

Bess smiled when she saw her frog then frowned again when she noticed Hazel.

Hazel lifted the domed lid of the time machine.

"Froggenstein can come, but you can't," Bess yelled. She put her nose in the air and held out her hand for Hazel to give her the small plastic aquarium.

Hazel didn't listen and instead sat down beside her sister, strapping herself in.

She could tell Bess was still mad. She had every right to be. "I'm sorry!" Hazel said over the sound of the time machine.

"You should be," Bess yelled back.

"I should've stood up to Bobby sooner" Hazel yelled back. "I should've been a better sister."

She reached over and gave Bess a hug, relieved when Bess finally softened up and hugged her back, even though it took her forever and only seemed like half a hug. The scratchy fabric of Bess's green sparkly outfit scraped Hazel's cheek, and she knew it was probably full of frog germs, but she didn't care. She was glad to have her sister back, and glad to be about to go on another adventure with her, even though they were supposed to wait to go until their grandfather gave them the wink.

The girls looked up from their hug and noticed a figure staring at them from across the room. The figure had a ball cap. *Oh no! Not Bobby!*

Hazel couldn't believe he had really followed her into the house — and into the attic! She would never enter someone else's house without asking first. That went against everyone's rules... and maybe even the law.

"What in the world?" the figure said.

Bess closed the lid of the time machine and smirked at Bobby. She swirled her hand wildly through the air, and hit a button on the control panel.

There was no time to worry about their new friend or the fact they were supposed to wait until Grandpa gave them the winking signal.

A bright light flashed.

Blip. They were gone.

*And Bobby had seen everything!*

# Chapter Seven

Hazel opened her eyes, but it was still dark. A cold wind blew up and around her cheeks from the opened hatch of the time machine. Goosebumps ran down her arms as the smell of mud and leaves filled the air. It was night time, and they were outside.

She turned her head this way and that, trying to find any signs of her sister. A branch from a nearby bush scratched at her nose, and she pushed it away. They had landed in the bushes again, but where was

Bess? And where were they?

Something told her not to call out her sister's name. It was dark and unusually quiet. Hazel pushed her way free from the branches and the time machine, walking out to what looked like a small footpath in the woods somewhere, but she couldn't tell for sure. All she could really see was darkness.

The stars and moon overhead were the only lights, and Bess was nowhere to be found. Had she run away and left her?

She couldn't still be mad about Froggenstein, could she? Hazel was the one who rescued her frog.

An owl hooted in a nearby tree, and Hazel jumped, almost tripping on a root under her feet. It was cold and she was scared. She felt her nose stuffing up and her eyes welling into tears. She wiped them away with her arm and looked around. She needed to be strong, find her sister, and figure this out.

Hazel took a deep breath and tried to think of a plan. She could see a path through the woods, but she knew that before she went anywhere, she needed to make sure she'd be able to find her way back to the time machine again. But in the dark of night, and with the bushes that surrounded it, the time machine was almost impossible to see.

Hazel pulled out the ribbon from her perfectly combed bun, and tied it around a branch of the bush where the time machine was. She stepped back and watched it wave to her crazily in the wind. She hoped she'd be able to see it again. She hoped it wouldn't blow off the branch. She knotted it around the branch one more time just to make sure. Good. It was definitely easy to see, even though in the dark of night, she couldn't even tell it was red.

She still couldn't believe Bess had really left her, but then, why was she surprised? Her sister never thought anything through before she did it. Never.

"B-B-Bess!" she whisper-called into the night. "Where are you?"

The wind picked up. She hugged her arms tightly around her body to keep warm. It was almost freezing cold and her sister was in a little fairy outfit. Hazel vaguely remembered her grandfather telling her to dress in warm clothes and wear good walking shoes. Poor Bess was in little ballet flats.

Hazel thought about walking the small trail to see if she could find Bess, but what if she went the wrong way? What if Bess was looking for her? Hazel sat down in the cold dirt of the path and tucked her head into her knees.

Something slimy and cold touched the back of Hazel's neck. *What in the world?* She reached behind her and felt something squishy and damp...

Rrrrrrr-ibbbbbetttt!

Hazel quickly turned around, looking up and into the eyes of her sister's frog. A dark figure in a fairy outfit stood over her, holding Froggenstein and laughing. Hazel had never been happier to have frog germs smeared all over her in her entire life. She stood up and went to hug her sister, but remembered at the last second that she should be mad at her. "Bess, you scared me! Where were you? Were you hiding? That wasn't funny!"

Bess put her frog back in his aquarium. Then she put the aquarium in the cloth bag she was carrying. "I heard voices. There are people walking this path. A whole group of them. I followed them, but I came back for you..."

"Well, that was nice of you," Hazel said, sarcastically.

Bess pulled on Hazel's arm. "Come on! We've got to catch up." She pointed to her feet. She was clomping around in oversized dark brown boots. "I already have the shoes Grandpa gave us, and the bread Grandma made us is in the bag." Crumbs fell from her face when she said that last part. Bess took off quickly up the path. She could move pretty fast in oversized shoes, but then, she was used to playing dress up.

"You better have saved me some of that bread," Hazel said, running to catch up.

Hazel could see a large group of people just ahead of them in the shadows of the trees. Were they really about to follow a group of strangers walking a dark wooded path at night? Hazel wasn't sure this was a good idea, but she really didn't have any other plan.

# Chapter Eight

Cold, dead leaves crunched under Hazel's feet as she and Bess scrambled to catch up to the group. She could hear them talking even though they were whispering ahead of her.

"I know you're cold, and I know you're tired, but when we get to Mr. Garrett's house, we'll all be able to rest. He'll give us warm food and new shoes..." a woman's voice said.

In the moonlight, Hazel could see

them clearly. Six people staggered along the path ahead of them, two women in long dresses and four men in tattered pants that barely covered their ankles. They all had dark hair and dark skin, with a small man in a hat walking in front of them, motioning with his arm like he was leading them someplace. Hazel wasn't sure if she and Bess should be hiding from the group or trying to get their attention. She decided she would try not to make much noise, just in case.

Rrrrrrrrrrrrribbbbbbbbet!

Of course her sister would have the loudest frog on Earth.

The man leading the group looked around and stopped. He put his arms out to stop the group behind him. Slowly, they turned around and faced the girls.

Hazel swallowed hard. Were they going to be mad about being followed?

"Hello," Bess said, waving and walking up to them.

The man leading the group threw the girls a relieved, warm smile. "You almost scared us to death, little ones."

Hazel saw the leader's face and heard his high-pitched voice. That wasn't a man! It was a woman dressed in men's clothing.

The woman stared at the girls for a second then shook her head. "What are you two wearing? You'll catch your death of cold in whatever that is. Walking around the woods of Delaware in the middle of a freezing cold night in..." the woman walked over to Bess and felt the fabric of her dress-up costume. "What kind of material is this, anyway? And why do you have wings?"

Bess laughed. "I'm a fairy," she said, shivering and rubbing her hands along her bare arms. "But a very cold one."

The woman laughed too. She immediately took off the thick gray coat she was wearing and motioned for the largest man in the group to do the same. They both handed them to Hazel and Bess.

"Oh thank you," the girls both said. Hazel wrapped herself in the scratchy warm fabric of the extra-large coat, but watched as her sister struggled to put hers on over her wings.

*Why did Bess always have to wear costumes?*

Hazel tried to get up enough courage to ask the group where they were headed and what they were doing, but she wasn't sure how to do it, so she just stood there, watching her sister struggle with the coat.

Bess pulled her wings off and stuck her hand out to the leader of the group. "I'm Bess and this is my sister, Hazel," she said. "Who are you guys, and where are we all going?"

The woman turned her head to the side, giving Bess and Hazel a suspicious look. "You girls look nice enough, but how do we know we can trust you? Where are your parents?"

The large man squatted down so he was the same height as Bess. "Yeah, we don't get too many cold fairies around here. Where did you girls say you were from and why are you dressed in those outfits?"

Hazel knew what was coming next. She looked over at her sister and shook her head, trying to hint to Bess not to tell them they were from the future. But she knew, Bess never listened to hints.

"Oh us? We're from the future. That's where our family's at," Bess said, buttoning the humungous coat. "I'm dressed like this because it was summer where we came from." She finished buttoning the coat then put her wings on over it. The coat almost dragged the ground.

The group looked at the girls like they were big green monsters with big snotty noses.

"That's a crazy story," one of the men said.

"My family's full of crazy stories," Bess said.

The woman laughed a little. "I've got some crazy stories myself. My name's Harriet. I won't tell you anyone else's name, just in case you can't keep a secret. Come on." She motioned for the group to start walking again. "We've got to keep moving, but you can come with us, seeing how your fairy family is stuck in the future."

Harriet made her way to the front of the group and began walking again. Bess and Hazel ran to catch up to her. Hazel could tell by the way the group was eyeing her and her sister that they didn't trust them, but she wasn't sure why.

"Why are there so many secrets? Why are we walking at night?" Hazel asked when they caught up to Harriet. "Why are we whispering?"

Harriet lowered her voice even further. "Because what we're doing is against the law, that's why. And we can't get caught."

Hazel gulped.

*Did she just say they were breaking the law?* Hazel never even broke the rules.

# Chapter Nine

Hazel's breath hung in front of her like a little frozen cloud. A chill ran down her spine even though she was in a nice, warm coat. She'd never done anything illegal before, and she wasn't about to start now. These people couldn't be the people they were supposed to help. Her grandparents wouldn't want them to help criminals!

"Excuse me, Ma'am," she whispered to the leader of the group as she looked around to make sure no one else could hear her. "Did you just say what we're doing right now is against the law?"

The woman stopped and looked at Hazel like she was crazy. "Some laws," the woman said, "are meant to be broken. That's the only way you can change them. The five people you see walking behind us are on the road to freedom. We're almost there, too. They are escaping slavery, and I'm helping them."

Bess almost stumbled in the long coat she was wearing. "What's slavery?" she asked. "And how do we escape it?"

Harriet's eyes sparkled in the moonlight. "I guess they must not have slavery in the future," she said, winking like she really didn't believe Bess's story about being from the future. "And that's a good thing. But I'll tell you what it is right now, here in the year 1849. In some states, like the one we're in, it's legal for people to own people. That's what slavery is. We're forced to work for someone else but we don't get paid because we're owned by them. How would you like to be owned by somebody — sold, rented out, have your family split apart, and treated terribly? Just terribly. And all because the color of your skin is darker."

"Oh," Bess said, turning her head to the side. "I'm sorry. That sounds awful."

"It is. That's why we've got to change the law by going against it." She started walking again. "And once we get into Pennsylvania where slavery is illegal, we'll all be safe," she said.

"How does that work?" Hazel asked.

"Just crossing over to another state means you'll be safe?"

"Right now, it does," Harriet said. "Once we cross into the Northern states where slavery is illegal, the laws will protect us, and we'll be free."

"There'd better be warmth and food soon," the large man who gave Hazel his coat said. "Or we won't make it to freedom. How much longer?"

Harriet chuckled. "Oh, it's just around the bend now."

"Harriet, you've been saying that for days," the man whisper-yelled. "We're all starving. We haven't eaten since yesterday."

Bess pulled open her bag, and the group stopped walking. The smell of freshly baked bread filled the night. "I just remembered my grandmother made this bread," she said, handing out loaves. The group eagerly, and thankfully, took the bread and dug in.

Hazel grabbed a piece, too. When she first got to the farmhouse, she hated her grandmother's homemade cooking, but it sure tasted good now.

"Delicious," the woman in charge kept saying. "Just what we needed."

Hazel looked at the woman, and gasped.

"What's the matter?" Bess asked, handing out more bread.

"I think this Harriet must be Harriet Tubman. She's famous," Hazel said, biting into piece of bread.

She'd read a book about Harriet Tubman once. She was one of the most famous people who helped escaping slaves on the Underground Railroad. She'd always pictured the woman being large and gruff, but this woman was smallish and friendly.

"So this is the Underground Railroad?" Hazel asked.

"Yes. Welcome aboard," Harriet chuckled.

"Thank Goodness," Bess said. She stopped and leaned against a tall oak tree. "I thought we were going to have to walk the entire way or something. When's the next train coming?"

Hazel shook her head. "No, Bess. The Underground Railroad isn't an actual railroad. It's what they called the route escaping slaves took to get to freedom, and all the people who helped along the way. We're passengers on the Underground

Railroad right now."

"So, I suppose I'm your conductor," Harriet said.

Bess turned her head to the side. "I still don't get it. Why don't we just take a train if there really are trains? It'd be quicker."

"Yes, there are trains," Harriet said. "But very few slaves escape using them. Once a slave gets reported missing, fliers are posted all around and rewards are set for catching them. It's never long before the police and the bounty hunters start watching train stations."

"So people are looking for you all right now?" Hazel asked, looking around, wondering if they were being watched.

"That's why we need to keep moving, and keep quiet."

The group picked up the pace. Hazel's feet ached and her legs felt like they were going to fall off, but she knew she hadn't even been walking that long. Had these poor people really been walking for days?

Just when she was about to tell the others that she needed a rest, they came across a large white two-story house with lots of windows, and Harriet told them this was their next stop. It had been a long walk through the woods, and Hazel was a little nervous about how they were going to make it back to their time machine in the dark of night by themselves when it was time to go home. She knew she couldn't ask Harriet or one of the others to go back with them. She couldn't ask them to go back when they were so close to freedom.

As Harriet approached the door, she

motioned for everyone in the group to hide in the nearby bushes that surrounded the house.

"Why do we have to hide?" asked Bess, a little too loudly.

"In case bounty hunters or the police are here,"one of the men said, shushing her.

"And, they might not want us," another said.

"They wouldn't send us away, would they?" Hazel asked, hugging the coat a little tighter. It was cold and she couldn't imagine how they'd all survive if they had to stay outside much longer.

"Yep," said a woman from the back. "It's happened before. If there are too many of us, or if the owner of the house has been harassed by the police, they might not want to take the risk."

From the bushes, they could hear the conversation at the door.

"Who is it?" a man's loud, angry voice asked. Hazel gasped. She had a bad feeling about this.

# Chapter Ten

Hazel's heart raced. She thought about her grandfather, remembering that just because a person had a grumpy voice and an angry expression didn't mean they were a bad person. And sometimes people with large smiles, compliments, and soccer balls weren't the nicest...

Hazel felt terrible, thinking about the way she and her new friend had treated Bess earlier in the day. Hazel had only wanted to play with someone other than her sister for a while, someone she didn't have to watch and be responsible for. She didn't mean to hurt her sister's feelings.

"Who is it?" the voice asked again, even louder, and angrier, this time.

"A friend with friends," Harriet whispered.

The door swung wide open, and a large man with white fluffy hair and a thick black suit smiled out into the night. "It's about time you got here," he said as he and Harriet greeted each other. "I've been worried about you all."

Harriet gestured for everyone to come inside. The house was warm with a fire going in the large fireplace against the back wall, and amazing smells came from the kitchen. An orangish yellow hue flickered off the hanging lanterns, causing shadows to dance across the walls and the furniture. Hazel remembered Harriet said it was the year 1849, and she remembered from her last trip in the time machine that indoor lighting wasn't possible until the late 1800s.

Most of the group took off their coats and warmed themselves against the fire as Harriet introduced them all to her good friend, Thomas Garrett. "If I'm the conductor of this Underground Railroad you're talking about, then this is a station master, and this house is a station."

A thin woman in a long dark dress hustled in from the kitchen, carrying a pot of soup and some bowls. Her hair was covered in a dark black bonnet. Hazel guessed she was Mr. Garrett's wife. The woman stopped short, almost dropping the pot when she saw the girls standing in the middle of the living room. Her mouth popped open and her eyes widened. "Harriet, who are these children?"

"Oh, we're just hungry, cold fairies from the future," Bess said, laughing so hard she almost stumbled in the large boots she was still wearing.

The woman got everyone started on their soup then took Harriet aside. Even though she was whispering, Hazel could still hear what she was saying.

"I don't think it's safe to bring unknown children to our house. What if they tell people?"

"And so what if they do tell people?" Mr. Garrett interrupted in the loudest voice Hazel had ever heard. "I've never made any secret about my feelings on slavery. It's wrong, and I don't care how many friends I lose or fines I have to pay. When someone is hurting someone else, the easiest thing to do in life is to turn your back and pretend you don't see it. It takes courage to help people and do what's right."

Hazel gulped, thinking about soccer balls, frogs, and the way she had treated her own sister.

Mr. Garrett went to his closet and brought out a large bin full of boots and other shoes. "Try these on and pick out the ones that'll work for you," he said to the group. "I've got all sizes, women's shoes too."

Everyone stopped eating and eagerly looked through the box, trying on shoe after shoe, smiling and laughing. It was the happiest Hazel had seen the group since they started.

Mr. Garrett turned back to his wife. "And think of Harriet. Harriet goes down to the South time and time again. She doesn't need to do that. She's already free from slavery. But she risks that freedom and her life to go down across the border in the dead of night to help others. Now that's real courage. I wouldn't be surprised if she became famous someday."

"She will be, or at least that's what my sister says," Bess said, barely looking up from the soup she was slurping. Messy drips fell all over the table as she ate. "And I think I heard about her in school last year."

Everyone who was busy trying on shoes in front of the fire stopped and looked over at Bess like she was crazy.

Hazel shook her head. Her sister was always saying the wrong things.

"See Harriet," Mr. Garrett said, putting his hand on Harriet's shoulder and chuckling. "It has to be true if a fairy from the future says it."

Harriet laughed too. "Oh no. I don't do any of this to be famous."

The sound of new shoes being tested along the wooden floor planks of Mr. Garrett's large house echoed throughout the living room. Most everyone had found a suitable pair from the shoe bin. Everyone except the large man who had given Hazel his jacket to wear earlier in the night.

"Do you have any shoes that'll fit me?" he asked Mr. Garrett.

Mr. Garrett looked around. "I used to have a large pair. Whatever happened to them?"

Hazel suddenly remembered the boots on her sister's feet, the ones their grandfather had given them to return to history.

"Are these the ones you're looking for?" Bess asked, pulling them off her feet. They clunked on the floor in front of her.

"How did you get them?" he said, snatching the boots. He held them up to the light of one of the lanterns. "These are my boots. How long have you had them?"

"She's been wearing them all night," one of the men in the group said.

Bess pulled out her ballet flats from the cloth bag and slipped them on. "These are my real shoes. They go with my fairy outfit."

Mr. Garrett took the cloth bag from

Bess's hands. "What else did you steal? Explain yourself. Did you girls break into my house and steal my boots?"

Hazel's throat felt dry and she couldn't speak. But worse, she had completely forgotten what her grandfather told her to say about the boots.

## Chapter Eleven

Mr. Garrett's eyes were beady and angry, very much like her grandfather's. "I asked you a question, young lady. Where did you get these shoes?"

Hazel tried to have courage. "We didn't steal them," she said. "It-It's just I can't seem to remember where we got them from."

Bess stood up. She looked especially small in the large coat she was still wearing. "Remember?" she said to Hazel. "We found them just outside, in a box on the porch as we were coming in."

Mr. Garrett looked off at the wooden beams in the ceiling like he was trying to remember something. He laughed. "I'm sorry," he said. "You're absolutely right. That *is* where I left them. I was cleaning them yesterday. I'm forgetting things in my old age."

"I'm forgetting things too," Hazel said, giving her sister a huge hug. Her oversized wool coat scratched against Hazel's face, but she didn't care. "Thanks for remembering," she whispered to her sister.

Rrrrrrrrrrriiiiiiiibbbbbbet!

"That was not what I was expecting to be in your bag," Mr. Garrett said, pulling Froggenstein's case out. "You'll have to forgive me for being a bit paranoid. We have to watch our backs around here." He held Froggenstein's aquarium up to the light. "What a nice frog. I used to catch frogs when I was about your age too."

Bess smiled smugly at Hazel. "See. I'm not too little to take care of a frog."

"I know," Hazel said. "I'm sorry I let Bobby make you feel that way. You're actually the perfect age to start taking care of things."

"And are you sorry for saying that it's no fun to watch me? I heard you say that to Bobby," she said.

No wonder Bess had been so mad. Hazel pulled her sister in closer. "I should never have said that. I've had the most fun ever hanging out with you this summer."

Soft morning light streamed in

through the window, and Hazel began to worry about the time. Their mother would be looking for them soon, and now that it was light, it was probably a good time to head home.

She also worried about their new friend and what he had done after seeing her and Bess disappearing in the time machine.

Ugh! What if he told his mom, or worse, what if he told their mom too?

Hazel nudged her sister. "Now that the sun's coming up, I think we'd better go home," she said to Bess.

"Yes," Mr. Garrett said. "It's probably time for our guests to rest up for the next leg of their journey into Pennsylvania and freedom. Soon, you will all have a new life."

Bess thanked Harriet for her coat,

finally taking it off and handing it back to her. Then she put Froggenstein in the bag, and slipped her glittery fairy wings back on over her costume.

After saying good-bye and thanking everyone for everything they'd done to help, the girls left into the chill of the morning. Hazel hated leaving her new friends and the warmth of the fire, but she knew it was time. After Mr. Garrett closed the door and couldn't hear her anymore, she turned to Bess. "Now," she said. "We need to remember where we put that time machine."

A foggy cold mist covered the ground. Hazel scanned the woods, trying to find the trail that would take them back to the time machine, but nothing seemed like it could be it.

"Do you know where you're going?" Bess asked, shivering.

"Of course," Hazel replied, even though she had no clue.

After searching a while, she finally thought she saw what looked like the trail, and she motioned for her sister to follow her. But Hazel still wasn't sure it was right. The trees all looked the same, and she couldn't see her ribbon yet.

"W-w-we're never gonna find it," Bess said, her teeth chattering from the cold.

"Don't worry," Hazel replied as confidently as she could muster. "It's just around the bend now." Birds chirped overhead and the sun was getting stronger as they walked along the path. "Besides, it'll get warmer soon, and I marked the way with my bright red hair ribbon. What could go wrong?"

Just then the girls heard galloping horses and angry voices over the calming sounds of the morning.

"I think they went this way!" a man's voice said. "Those slaves are not getting away. Not this time."

*Oh no! Could they be bounty hunters?*

Hazel pulled her sister into a nearby bush to hide. She peeked out just as two men on horseback went by, looking off in all directions. And one of them was carrying her bright red ribbon! *Oh no!*

# Chapter Twelve

Hazel pointed to the men as they galloped by. "Did you see that?" she whispered.

"Yeah," Bess replied, adjusting her thick glasses. "What in the world is that guy going to do with your hair ribbon? Put his hair into a bun?" She laughed so hard she snorted.

"What was that noise?" The man with the ribbon asked, tugging gently on the reins of his horse so he could turn around and head back in the direction of the girls.

Hazel shushed her sister. Her heart raced, and she no longer cared that she was cold. Slowly, the men made their way back toward the girls.

Hazel lowered her voice even farther. "I think they're bounty hunters."

"What?"

"Shhhh, Bess, you have to be quiet. Bounty hunters are people who look for escaping slaves so they can get money for turning them in."

Bess's eyes looked as big as dinner plates behind her thick glasses. "We can't let them go near Mr. Garrett's."

Hazel grabbed her sister and yanked her into the middle of the trail. "You're right. Come on," she shouted, running in all directions, but as far away from the house as she could.

Bess followed. "I thought we needed to be quiet."

"No, Bess. This time we actually need to be as loud as we can!"

Bess grinned. "Say no more," she yelled, running and jumping through the woods like a crazy fairy. "That's my specialty!"

Just as they'd hoped, the bounty hunters chased after them, getting farther and farther away from Mr. Garrett's house and the escaping slaves.

Hazel's heart pounded in her t-shirt and it was hard for her to catch her breath, but she tried to keep running. Branches scratched at her arms and she couldn't tell one tree from the next. She and Bess were fooling the bounty hunters, all right, but they were getting even more lost in the process. How were they ever going to get home now? The ribbon wasn't on the tree in front of the time machine anymore.

Out of breath, Hazel finally stopped and leaned against one of the trees. Bess stopped too.

"I don't know where we're at," Hazel admitted through gasps of breath. They had run so far into the woods, she no longer saw any signs of the makeshift trail anymore.

It didn't take long for the men on horseback to catch up to the girls. But when they saw who they were following, their faces dropped into disappointment. "I can't believe we've been chasing a couple of kids playing in the woods," one of the men said, throwing Hazel's ribbon down in the dirt.

"We thought they were slaves."

"I guess we know who owns that weird, fancy toy we saw back there, the one that was marked by the ribbon," the other man said, pointing off toward a patch of bushes off the trail. "I wonder what kind of toy it was, anyway. I've never seen anything like it."

"Who cares if we can't get money for it? Let's go home."

Hazel finally caught her breath when she saw the men leave. As soon as it was safe, she picked up her ribbon and followed the direction the man had pointed, relieved to see their weird, fancy "toy" again.

She and Bess quickly jumped into the time machine and strapped themselves in, carefully waiting to turn anything on until they were absolutely sure no one was going to hear them. A bright light flashed. Blip. They were gone.

# Chapter Thirteen

As if she were waking from a dream, Hazel slowly opened her eyes. Someone was calling her name.

"Hazel! Hazel! Wake up!"

Hazel blinked her eyes and forced them to focus. Messy blonde hair and a bright green fairy outfit...

"Come on!" Bess said, tugging on Hazel's arm. "Mom's calling us!"

Hazel looked around the attic — at the bookcase, the boxes of rusty mechanical parts, and the old familiar army trunk. She was happy to be back in the safety of the stuffy hot attic of the farmhouse again. She stood up. Her cute white shoes were covered in dirt from the trail out to the time machine where bounty hunters had chased her and Bess moments before, but she didn't care.

She hoped Harriet Tubman, Mr. Garrett, and the escaping slaves were going to be okay. But Hazel thought she remembered her teacher saying that Harriet Tubman never lost even one passenger as a conductor on the Underground Railroad, so she knew the whole group was going to be just fine.

"Girls! Girls! Come down here this instant," their mother called from downstairs. Judging from her tone, the girls knew she wasn't happy. "Bobby is here with his mother, and they have a lot of questions!"

Hazel gasped, remembering earlier in the day when their new friend had watched them leave in the time machine. She took a deep breath. It was time to see what had happened.

Bess raced down the stairs, and Hazel went to follow her, but she tripped on one of the boxes stacked along the sides of the garage. The box spilled over, and old pictures and papers scattered everywhere. Hazel looked at her hand. It was covered in dusty cobwebs. She tried not to think about it, and the millions of other germs she probably also had from 1849. Ugh. She wiped her hand off on her shorts.

"Hazel! Hazel! Where are you?" her

mother called from downstairs.

"One second, Mom," Hazel replied, quickly picking up the box and stuffing the papers and pictures back into it. Old black and white photos of ancestors she never knew smiled up at her. There were also pictures of her grandparents, and some of her mother as a kid. One caught her eye. In the photo, her mother was a little girl, eating cotton candy in front of a familiar domed lid — with a closed green army trunk by her feet.

*This photo must've been taken the day of the fair!* The day when something terrible happened. *The family secret!*

Since their mother already knew the time machine and the trunk full of antiques existed, why couldn't they talk to her about it? What had happened the day of the fair?

Hazel quickly searched the box for other pictures from that day, for other clues. She wondered if she could use the photo to start up the time machine and go back in time to that exact day. Then she could see for herself what had happened.

She ran a finger along the edge of the old photo. *Would she really do that?*

"Honestly, Hazel! If you don't come down, I'm coming up. What are you up to?" Her mother yelled, her voice growing nearer.

# Chapter Fourteen

Hazel threw the photo into the box, put the lid back on, and ran down the stairs before her mother could call her again. She decided she'd come back later to look through the box again as soon as she got the chance.

Whatever had happened that day so long ago was the reason her grandparents had changed jobs and moved to the country, while her mother refused to talk about it.

She was still thinking about the time machine and the secret when she caught up to Bess, who was standing in the living room, holding her pet frog. Across the room, their mother sat on the couch next to Bobby and a large woman with glasses. She introduced Hazel to the woman. "Susie, this is my oldest, Hazel. Hazel, this is Bobby's mother and my old friend, Mrs. Jacobs."

Bobby stood up and pointed when he saw Hazel. "Tell my mom, Hazel. You took my frog and then you... you and your sister... they both disappeared! One second they were there in the attic, and the next second they were gone."

Hazel held in her gasp, telling herself not to panic even though things were just as bad as she'd thought. He had told everyone. She looked over at Bess. Bess just shrugged.

"Poor kid's been saying that all day," their grandfather said, as he casually walked in from the kitchen, biting into one of their grandmother's homemade rolls. "I sent him home and told him to go lie down for a while. He's acting crazy if you ask me. He's not crazy, is he?" He turned to Bobby's mother.

"I'm sorry, Susie," their mother said.

"I'm not crazy. I saw what I saw," Bobby said. "And I saw those two disappear! Hazel ran into the house and I followed her in. There was a loud noise coming from the attic, so I went upstairs..."

"Wait a second," his mother snapped, adjusting her glasses and sitting up in her seat. "You went into someone else's house and up into their attic without their permission?"

Bobby's face grew red under his freckles. "I...uh... that's not the point. You and Hazel's mom are friends. And, the important part is I saw them disappear. Come on, Hazel. Tell my mom how you and your sister disappeared."

Hazel shook her head. "I don't know what you're talking about. But then, older kids sometimes have crazy imaginations."

*Rrrrrrrrrrrriiiiiiiiiiiiibbbbbbbbet!*

Seeing the frog, Bobby ran over to Bess. He grabbed Froggenstein's aquarium out of her hand. "And here's proof. This is my frog. I taught the girls how to play soccer, and they gave me the frog. But then, they took it back, so I had to go into the house to get it."

"Nope," Hazel said, grabbing the cage and giving it back to her sister. "This has always been Bess's frog and it always will be Bess's frog."

Bobby scowled. "I thought you were cool," he said.

Bess gave Hazel a hug. "She is," she said. Hazel hugged her little sister back. Sure, having a friend her own age was fun, but not if it meant she couldn't be friends with her sister.

Bobby's mother stood up to leave. "I'm so sorry for all the problems Bobby has caused today. Honestly, I don't know what's gotten into him," she said. "It's just so crazy."

Hazel's grandfather went back into the kitchen, winking at the girls as he left. "Crazy, all right. Just crazy."

On the way out the door, Bobby looked back. He pointed two fingers at the girls to let them know he was watching them. And somehow Hazel knew he meant it. This definitely wasn't going to be the last time they saw their curious new friend. But right now, she had more important things to think about like helping their grandpa return stolen stuff to their places in history, investigating the mysterious box full of photos, and the secret. Hazel had no idea how she was going to do any of that stuff right now, but she knew deep down, she finally had the courage to do them all.

## — The End —

Hi. Thank you so much for reading my book. I hope you liked reading it as much as I liked writing it. And if you did, please consider telling your friends about it and leaving a review.

Here are the other books in the Time Machine Girls series if you're interested:

Book One: Secrets
Book Two: Never Give Up
Book Three: Courage
Book Four: Teamwork

And if you'd like to know more about me, or the books I write, please go to my website www.ernestinetitojones.com.  You can also join my list there to know when new books are coming out.

Read on for more about Harriet Tubman and the Underground Railroad.

Thanks again!
Ernestine Tito Jones

## More About Harriet Tubman
## And the Underground Railroad

When I was a kid learning about the
Underground Railroad, I was like Bess. I thought it
was an actual railroad. My history books didn't
include a lot of information about it or slavery, so I
was pretty confused. I wrote this book because I
wanted to learn more about it, and help others
who might be confused about it too. And while
researching it, I was amazed at the courage of
everyone involved — from the people escaping
slavery to the people helping them do it. These
courageous people helped change the laws of the
United States.

Slavery is a hard subject to talk about because
we can't imagine it now. Simply put, people used
to own people. They forced them to work in their
fields and in their houses. Slaves were often
treated terribly. Sometimes, they were beaten and
killed. They were sold and loaned out like
property. Families were split apart. And the only
difference between the slave and the person who

owned the slave was usually the color of the person's skin. These are all concepts that are hard to understand now, and they should be. But it's still important to talk about what happened, and honor the people who helped to change it.

Slavery in the United States lasted until 1865, and this story takes place toward the end of it in 1849. No one is really sure when people along the Underground Railroad started referring to themselves in railroad terms, but the Underground Railroad is just what they called it when escaping slaves received help on their route to freedom. They usually escaped by foot (not on a train, or even along a railroad track, which was what I thought when I was a kid) and these people hid out in houses along the way. They went from the South (where slavery existed) to the North (where it did not). Once slaves made it to the North, they had immediate freedom there because the laws protected them. The "railroad" was called "underground" because it was a secret. It wasn't really under ground. When people say something is "underground," sometimes that just means it's hidden. Everyone on the Underground Railroad was going against the law, so they had to keep things a secret. That's why records weren't kept as well as with other things. It's why we don't know very much about the people along the Underground Railroad.

## What Do These Railroad Terms Mean, Anyway?

Because we don't ride on trains as much as we used to, these railroad terms are kind of confusing to us now. Here's what they mean.

**Conductor**: A conductor on a railroad is a person who runs the train. Harriet Tubman was a conductor on the Underground Railroad because she went down to the South, gathered a group of slaves who wanted to escape, and led them (usually by foot but not always) to the safe houses along the way to freedom.

**Stations:** Stations along a railroad are the stops a train makes. The stations along the Underground Railroad were usually just the houses and stores that escaping slaves could stay at along the route. They received food, warmth, shelter, and supplies.

**Station Master:** A station master on a real railroad is the person who runs the station. In the

Underground Railroad, station masters were the owners of the houses and stores that the escaping slaves relied on to help them gain their freedom. Both white people and free black people helped escaping slaves gain their freedom by housing them along the Underground Railroad. Thomas Garrett was a station master.

**Passengers:** Escaping slaves were the "passengers" on the Underground Railroad.

**Codes:** Because things had to be kept secret, codes were used a lot of the time. Slaves used code words, usually sung in songs and hymns to communicate with each other about escaping. Conductors used codes when approaching a station, saying things like "It's a friend with friends."

**Bounty hunters:** When slaves escaped, the people who "owned" them would offer a reward for their return. Bounty hunters made their living looking for escaping slaves and other people escaping the law.

### What's True in this Story?

Harriet Tubman and Thomas Garrett really were friends who helped each other out on the

Underground Railroad as a conductor and a station master. Thomas Garrett really did give shoes, food, money, and shelter to as many escaping slaves as he could.

In this story, though, bounty hunters chased Bess and Hazel, nearly catching up to Harriet Tubman and her gang, but in reality, bounty hunters never got that close. Harriet was very good at what she did. She was a clever, resourceful conductor who knew her routes well and how to travel the woods safely. She never lost a passenger, which just means no one who went with her ever got caught or died along the way.

But that doesn't mean it was an easy passage to make. Often times they were cold, hungry, tired, and yes, even scared. Most times, they had to travel at night so they wouldn't get caught and didn't always have a place to sleep, so sometimes they had to sleep outside. Harriet became a free woman when she made it to Pennsylvania the first time. She didn't need to make the journey back to the South, but she did it many, many times just to help as many people as she could. When she wasn't helping on the Underground Railroad, Harriet worked in Pennsylvania (a free state) just to make enough money to go out and do it all over again. She gave her time, her money, and risked her life to help others on the Underground Railroad.

Imagine how hard it must have been to communicate a secret like this before there were phones and internet. But thousands of slaves were freed using the Underground Railroad. All the people who helped along the way risked their lives and their livelihoods (they could've been arrested, fined, jailed, or killed) because they were going against the law. But by doing so, they helped to change things.

Slavery was a huge issue at the time in the United States and caused the country to split into two distinct sections, the North and the South. This division led to the Civil War. After the war ended in 1865, slavery in the United States was officially abolished.

Made in the USA
Middletown, DE
30 September 2021